She Is Myth II

Ancel Mondia

Ukiyoto Publishing

All global publishing rights are held by

Ukiyoto Publishing

Published in 2024

Content Copyright © Ancel Mondia

ISBN 9789364943017

*All rights reserved.
No part of this publication may be reproduced,
transmitted, or stored in a retrieval system, in any form
by any means, electronic, mechanical, photocopying,
recording or otherwise, without the prior permission of
the publisher.*

The moral rights of the authors have been asserted.

*This book is sold subject to the condition that it shall not by
way of trade or otherwise, be lent, resold, hired out or
otherwise circulated, without the publisher's prior
consent, in any form of binding or cover other than that in
which it is published.*

www.ukiyoto.com

Contents

Mermaid	1
Dryad	5
Sphinx	8
Faery	12
Elf	16
Centaur	20
About the Author	*23*

Mermaid

In an area where salty water and rocky land physically met, a light and slow tune gently filled the windy atmosphere.

Rhythmic words clearly came out from the alluring lips of a fair and thin lady that was leisurely treading the typical coast.

She beautifully and heartfully sang perfect rhymes that apparently contained a profound message.

"Beneath the ocean breathes a mystery. She hands favor and she casts misery. Her beauty imprints in his memory. Departure is a burden to carry."

All of a sudden, a tan and muscly man appeared, with radiant happiness on his handsome face, right behind the fair and thin lady.

He instantly embraced her, as his strong arms tightly wrapped around her soft chest, and his front gently touched her back.

Extreme surprise obviously changed the calm facial expression of the comely lady.

However, when she swiftly looked over her smooth shoulder, her serene aura clearly returned.

The lady and the man sweetly exchanged stares that intensely contained their romantic love for each other.

She slowly turned to directly face him, and without audible words, their warm bodies naturally moved closer, and their reddish lips passionately kissed.

The normal silence of the typical coast was pleasurably replaced by sensual moans of the young lovers.

The lady steadily closed her charming eyes and mindlessly opened her enticing mouth, as the man fervently kissed her smooth neck.

He slowly caressed her covered breast, and quietly began to unbutton her plain dress.

Her nervous eyes abruptly opened, her gasping mouth strongly trembled, and her weak hands effortlessly pushed him away.

The tan and muscly man was obviously shocked as unexpected questions visibly contorted his handsome face.

"What is wrong, Mermaid, my love?" He blurted out.

Mermaid suddenly looked extremely confused, and her anxious eyes unsteadily looked at the pained man.

"I don't know, love. I don't know. But this doesn't feel right." She stuttered.

The man heavily sighed, instantly gave an understanding stare, and gently held Mermaid's thin arms.

"Don't be scared, my love. Come with me. Let's get married and live together. I'll provide for you and take care of you." He assuredly comforted her.

Mermaid reluctantly shook her head as her long hair was strongly blown by the invisible wind.

The man calmly extended his rough hand to remove Mermaid's hair that slightly covered her tear-stained face.

However, Mermaid abruptly resisted the man's loving touch, and extreme heartbreak weakened his masculine demeanor.

"I'm sorry, love. But my cowardice is too strong to overcome. Please, let me go." Mermaid begged.

The man desperately objected by forcibly attempting to carry the resisting lady, but powerful pity visibly showed in his teary eyes.

He slowly weakened his firm grasp and reluctantly let go of her, as he mindlessly looked at her dashing away from him.

He feebly fell to his trembling knees hurtfully pressed on the rocky land, as she gradually submerged in the salty water.

The windy atmosphere turned into stormy weather, as the heartbreaking separation took place on the typical coast.

Mermaid fully disappeared from the sight of the man, and all of a sudden, a wide fish's tail surfaced, splashed, and vanished.

Dryad

In a verdant woodland where towering tree canopies randomly overlapped, and haphazardly shaded the grassy ground, quietly stood a youthful and beautiful woman.

Her piercing eyes gradually closed, and in a short while, her peaceful face strongly contorted in visible fear and extreme pain.

She suddenly opened her eyes that overwhelmingly emitted indignation, and shakily parted her lips that menacingly uttered revenge.

"No one had ever dared inflict death on my home! The oak is mine! Anyone who braves to make it fall, shall fall into my hands."

For a split second, she mightily lifted her dainty feet, and wildly dashed into the verdant woodland where the light from the sky and the shadows of the trees seemingly competed for earthly space.

As the furious woman forcefully moved towards the center of the grassy ground, a roaring sound gradually grew louder in the tense air and stronger in her responsive ears.

All of a sudden, the speeding woman fully stopped, and large and heavy tears simultaneously dropped from her reddish and strained eyes.

Exactly in front of her, a huge and hard oak boomingly fell on the grassy ground, obviously from the fatal cut by a powerful chainsaw, tightly held by a sturdy man.

"No!!!" The woman screamed in deep agony.

In utter shock, the man abruptly turned his head, and saw the hysterical woman right behind him.

He subtly looked puzzled, and confusedly faced the seemingly insane woman.

"What's your problem, woman?" He arrogantly asked.

Upon hearing the masculine voice, the woman suddenly stared straight at the proud man.

The visible agony in her feminine demeanor gradually subsided and was taken over by extreme indignation.

"You cut down my oak. My oak is dead! Now, it's your turn to die!"

The retaliated woman speedily moved towards the agile man who skillfully defended himself by his solid chainsaw.

Abruptly the aggressive woman cunningly took a step back, and when she was about to visibly reattack, the focused man forcefully hurled the metal chainsaw at her.

The seemingly insane woman helplessly fell on the fallen oak trunk, and the youthful blood from her wounded body slowly dropped on the freshly cut tree.

"I am Dryad. No one can defeat me in my home." She whispered heavily.

The mad man was about to physically hit the fallen woman, when suddenly she and the tree horribly fused and formed into one existence.

The new terrible being proudly stood, and in extreme fear the man strongly appeared paralyzed.

Dryad wickedly approached the motionless man, leisurely lifted her veiny hands, and all at once, strangled him.

The sturdy man dropped dead on the grassy ground, and a horrifying laughter resoundingly hovered in the verdant woodland.

Sphinx

In a dry desert that was seldom wetted by rainfall, the daytime heat rapidly dropped into nightly chill, but a woman inhabitant of the sandy area intriguingly survived despite the absence of water.

She physically possessed a beautiful face of a typical lady, and a muscly body similar to a beastly lion.

She calmly moved her legs like a serpent in quietude, and proudly spread her arms as an eagle in power.

All of a sudden, the woman inhabitant paused, slowly turned her head, and her eyes strongly looked retaliated.

She steadily looked at the group of youthful men, treading the dry desert, and nearing her direction.

The youthful men obviously noticed the woman inhabitant, and their faces visibly had the same reaction of having discovered a mystery.

They hurriedly came closer to the woman inhabitant, and purposefully surrounded her, as she silently remained standing.

One of the men exclaimed. "Finally, we've found you!"

Another man inquisitively asked. "Is it real? That you are Sphinx?"

The man next to him insultingly said. "Can we wife you up?"

Altogether, the youthful men offensively laughed, but the woman inhabitant physically stayed motionless.

One of the men intuitively talked. "Oh, stop. She looks offended."

The man across from him proudly replied. "She's not. She enjoys getting a lot of attention from us. Right, Sphinx?"

He was about to visibly extend his hands to the woman inhabitant, when she obviously exposed her long and sharp fingernails, and he instantly stepped backward.

The intuitive man spoke again. "We heard that you speak in riddles. Your name has been highly talked about in our place. So we tried our luck, and found you here."

The woman inhabitant directly faced the intuitive man.

He humbly continued. "May we hear a riddle from you?"

She slowly looked at the youthful men physically surrounding her, as they obviously looked patiently anticipating a riddle from her.

A stern and deep voice audibly came out of her lips as she spoke.

"What walks on four legs in the morning, two legs in the afternoon, and three legs in the evening?"

The youthful men, except the intuitive one, simultaneously blurted out their answers.

Instantly the woman inhabitant ferociously attacked the youthful men, and they helplessly lost their lives.

The intuitive man strongly trembled in fear as he closely witnessed the youthful men violently devoured by the woman inhabitant.

All of a sudden, she steadily laid her retaliated eyes on his disconcerted appearance.

The intuitive man weakly opened his mouth and clearly uttered. "Man."

Instantly the horrific sandstorm visibly occurred a few meters behind the woman inhabitant.

She wordlessly stood and gradually stepped backward, as the mighty and sandy wind moved nearer to her.

As the woman inhabitant trod away from the intuitive man, she slowly transformed into a seemingly crossbreed creature.

Her human face physically remained, as her muscly body turned into the beastly lion.

A tail of the serpent in quietude, and wings of the eagle in power, slowly grew out of her back.

All of a sudden, the horrific sandstorm seemingly captured and wholly swallowed Sphinx as she totally disappeared in plain sight.

Faery

In a magical garden where flowering shrubs were harmoniously arranged, and narrow trees were artfully planted, stood a delicate and beautiful woman dressed in white clothing.

The natural hues of the flower garden appealingly blended and gracefully contrasted with one another, highlighting the benevolent presence of the mystical woman.

She obviously looked deeply amused upon delightfully beholding the multicolored mix of flowering shrubs and leisurely caressing the variegated group of narrow trees dreamily surrounding her.

Suddenly, the enchanting woman visibly paused when she consciously noticed the faint sound of footsteps nearby.

In a short while, her attentive ears clearly heard a snapping noise, and her composed face abruptly appeared tensed by conspicuous panic.

The disconcerted woman swiftly searched the magical garden, and directly perceived the average man tightly holding the freshly cut flower.

The offended woman firmly stared at the unknowing man, as her sharp eyes were apparently filled with a heavy accusation against the violator of nature.

The innocent man was about to physically leave the magical garden, when the mystical woman tamely spoke.

"Mister, can you stay a little longer?"

The average man was obviously surprised upon clearly hearing the soft and calm voice of the enchanting woman.

He shyly turned around and swiftly looked amused when his childlike eyes directly met the radiant eyes of the delicate and beautiful woman.

"How can I help you?" He naively asked.

She sweetly smiled as she meekly answered. "Don't you know, Mister? I'm the keeper of the garden."

The average man suddenly looked ignorant and puzzled, and the mystical woman gradually appeared stern and cold.

With a threatening husky voice, she spoke. "Do as I command, or you'll suffer the consequences."

The average man visibly trembled as he weakly threw the freshly cut flower tightly held by his rough hand.

With a begging voice, he said. "Forgive me. I didn't know what I've done. Please let me leave."

The offended woman slowly shook her head, and the regretful man submissively knelt and shamefully bowed his head.

The mystical woman sternly and coldly spoke. "Drink this, or you'll die."

The crying man reluctantly lifted his head, and unsteadily stared at the silver goblet directly handed to him.

He shakily extended his sweaty hands to hesitantly hold the gleaming glass.

The woman dressed in white, spoke in an offended voice. "Receive your punishment, or you'll never be free. No one escapes the wrath of Faery."

Upon clearly hearing the threatening husky words of Faery, the pitiable man visibly resolved to drink the unknown liquid contained by the silver goblet.

After he audibly gulped, his entire body involuntarily trembled, and all at once, he turned stone-dead.

Faery gradually restored her delicate and beautiful demeanor as translucent wings widely spread out of her back, as the magical garden swiftly appeared like the ideal fairyland filled with otherworldly insects and dreamy atmosphere.

Elf

In the tropical forest, on decaying logs and dying trunks, freely grew countless umbrella-shaped mushrooms with distinct colors from cream and yellow to pink and brown.

The obviously scattered forest wastes visibly breathed life to the flourishing fungal organisms with fleshy caps, short stalks, and several gills.

One misty morning, a tall and slender lady with fair complexion and beautiful face delightfully entered the tropical forest.

She leisurely danced with grace and magic, as the typical mushrooms surrounding her supernatural presence, perceivably lighted up with vibrance and life.

Her long loose dress luminously complemented her crystal and metal pieces of jewelry perfectly placed as her forehead chain, ear cuffs, and pendant necklace.

In a short while, the ethereal lady noticeably heard a gradually loudening rustle of dry leaves behind her.

She slowly had a knowing smile on her pinkish lips, and a sweet look on her grayish eyes.

She elegantly turned around and anticipatedly faced a seemingly ordinary man who slightly smiled at her in an instant.

The ordinary man clearly witnessed the conspicuous way that her eyes blinked and her heart beat at once.

She cheerfully embraced the ordinary man who reluctantly wrapped his typical arms around her delicate body.

"I miss you." The lady heartfully said.

The man weakly nodded and vacantly stared at the lady.

She excitedly entered her thin hand inside her side pocket, and gently pulled out a mystical object which appeared to be a handmade amulet.

The ethereal lady happily placed the powerful necklace on her pale palms and extended her slender arms to directly present her thoughtful gift to the ordinary man.

He slightly smiled, slowly shook his head, and calmly raised his rough hand to gently push her open hands.

The visible delight on her beautiful face suddenly turned to extreme sadness.

She weakly said. "I'm sorry if you don't like it. Will this lessen your love for me?"

He heavily sighed as he obviously looked anxious.

She sadly continued. "What is it? Tell me."

The man hesitantly replied. "This has nothing to do with you. It's me. I'm the problem."

The lady instantly comforted him. "You're not a problem. You're never a problem to me."

He quickly shook his head, and stared straight at her.

"I don't love you, Elf." He clearly admitted.

Elf was in extreme shock, as glistening tears perceivably came out of her pained eyes.

She deeply sobbed. "How can you do this to me?"

The man anxiously said. "Elf, I'm sorry."

Elf hurtfully cried. "All I wished for you was protection. But you only rejected me."

She madly looked at the handmade amulet in her trembling hands, and strongly pressed the mystical object with her veiny fingers.

All of a sudden, the powerful necklace visibly shattered, and her bitter tears simultaneously dropped on the seemingly dying mushrooms on the forest ground.

In an instant, the ordinary man painfully coughed, his entire body horribly trembled, and all at once he loudly drew his last breath.

Elf heartlessly stared at the dead man she once dearly loved, and nonchalantly turned her back.

Her ears suddenly grew long and pointed, and her entire being strongly radiated light.

Centaur

The chain of mountains of steep slopes, rugged terrains, and prominent peaks, was harmoniously inhabited by diverse species of plants and animals.

The frequent rainfall that naturally wetted the towering landform leisurely flowed all over the place, and into falls and streams nearby and beneath.

The harsh climate that was visibly carried by wind patterns and cool temperatures, constantly cleansed the environment to steadfastly sustain life.

Somewhere in the mountain forest, suddenly appeared two women with snappy movement and muscular physique.

They heatedly exchanged arrogant stares and mocking insults, and boldly faced each other with an air of rivalry.

"This is the moment of truth, Centaur. We'll see for ourselves who is stronger and faster between you and me." A woman threateningly spoke.

Centaur offensively smirked. "You'll be ashamed of all the bragging you did. You'll be sorry for every insult you gave me. You'll have a taste of your own medicine, Lady Nobody."

The woman rudely replied. "How bitter, Centaur! Walk your talk! Accept my challenge now. Through the woods, have a race with me. To see who is the first one to step on the peak."

Centaur proudly declared. "I accept the challenge. And I'll beat you."

The two women simultaneously crouched down, with both hands on the forest ground, and their back knee placed next to their front ankle.

In unison, they extended both knees as their body leaned forward, and in a split second, they speedily ran as if their very own life was at stake.

Centaur normally moved with extreme haste and visible pride, on the muddy ground and under the heavy rain.

She gradually smiled when her speeding feet strongly felt the more solid ground, and her muscular body wetted by thick raindrops, was dried up by the warm sun.

The bright view of the mountain peak got clearer as she ran closer towards the end of the race.

All of a sudden, Centaur slowed down and fully stopped from reaching the top, with a sense of shame and defeat on her face.

Right on the mountain peak, proudly stood her very own rival with an air of victory.

The woman harshly laughed. "Now, who is stronger and faster between us? Definitely, no other than me!"

Centaur retorted with overwhelming disbelief. "You cheated me!"

The woman gradually gave a cunning smile, and teasingly nodded.

Centaur appeared extremely retaliated, and from her waist down to her feet, horribly grew the flesh and fur of the horse.

She suddenly turned into a half-human and half-horse being, and speedily ran towards her shocked rival.

Centaur powerfully pushed the woman who helplessly fell from the mountain peak down to the unseen bottom, as Centaur proudly stood at the top of the chain of mountains.

About the Author

Ancel Mondia

Ancel Mondia is an NBDB-registered Ilongga writer, awarded as Fiction - Woman Writer of the Year 2023 by Ukiyoto Publishing, and a graduate of Master of Arts in English and Literature.

www.ingramcontent.com/pod-product-compliance
Lightning Source LLC
LaVergne TN
LVHW041643070526
838199LV00053B/3544